Coffee Time Tales

To David a Gemma

Very Best Wishes.

John Greene

Lowberry

D0452485

Coffee Time Tales
Description and Product List

Coffee Time tales is a collection of short stories with a twist of sugar or lemon to end them. Also there are a few poems, plus a participation story for children, read them the story and get them to repeat the vehicle noises you make, also one for you to finish called Mr Easy; read the story and then write your own ending from the information in the story. I have a number of endings in mind but what's yours? Email your answers to johngreene1947@yahoo.com or by mail to John Greene, c/o For The Right Reasons Publisher, 60, Grant Street, Inverness IV3 8BS.

It's a real mixture, some for fun, some for love and some for more sinister reasons. However nearly all of them have a hint or more of the seven deadly sins.

They are not meant to please everyone; I don't think anyone can but there just might be a section that you may enjoy and maybe see a little bit of yourself in some of the tales. Please don't sue me. If you do, I can't afford it.

None of the content is based on real people, circumstances or events and was not produced to offend anyone.

Other publications and products by John Greene, pen name Lowberry.

The Poetry Game (a book of my own poetry)
1. The Poetry Game (the second half, as above)
2. My Trip Home (an ancestral trip to Lowberry in Eire)
3. Live C.D. of my own poetry with music (taken from my two books)

Coffee Time Tales

CONTENTS

C. M. C. S. INC:

Coleman had been feeling unwell lately, just lethargic and run down. That will be running after his big boss man upstairs, he thought, as he pressed the toaster button. He went round the kitchen with cook, who herself glided across the stone floor with elegant grace, almost like a couple on the dance floor. They were just inches away at times, not in so many years, had they even touched, let alone collided, so pre-arranged was the routine. They steadily prepared breakfast for the boss.

From upstairs, they heard a door slam and footsteps across the first floor landing, then heavy footfall down the stairs.

"Coleman! Where the devil are you, man?" were the first words they heard.

Coleman sighed, and then uttered something unprintable before saying out loud. "Coming, Sir."

Coleman met his boss Brentford at the bottom of the stairs. "Good Morning Sir" he said.

"Coleman, I've got one hell of a day ahead of me and I've not had the best of starts, so just make sure that everything runs smoothly regarding breakfast." Then without drawing breath, he added "Has my paper arrived yet?"

"Yes Sir" replied Coleman."Your paper is in your study and breakfast is ready."

"Well man, get it served up, what are you waiting for?" said Brentford.

Coleman thought that Brentford Washington Blake was one of the richest men and just possibly the nastiest man on the planet.

Brentford made his way to the dining room, sat down and watched his maid pouring his morning coffee. He glanced quickly at her as she left the room and realised she had not said a word to him. No Good morning, nothing. Maybe she was still hurting over his approach to her the other day, when I asked her to spend the night with me. I was drunk, he thought. So what! She won't ignore me.

Just as he was about to call her, Coleman came in with his paper. He snatched it away and indicated in an impatient way by waving his arm at Coleman, dismissing him without a care or a word of thanks. He then proceeded to tuck into his breakfast delivered earlier by the cook.

Bastard, thought Coleman as he left the room. His breakfast finished, Brentford got up and went through to the hall. Coleman was waiting, coat ready for his boss to put on. Brentford stood, like the arrogant man that he was, as Coleman slipped the coat on his shoulders and then handed his boss his briefcase and hat.

No words were spoken as Coleman opened the door and Brentford walked out and down the steps to his waiting car and driver who stood with the rear door of the Limo open. He got in and as the driver fitted himself in the front seat behind the wheel. Brentford barked out his orders for where they were going. The drivers face said it all, another day of drudgery ahead.

Coleman meanwhile had closed the front door and feeling a little lighter on his feet, gave what could only be described as a little skip but he quickly regained his composure, and his stride, when he heard the dining room door open.

The young maid skipped herself across the lobby floor and with a loving motion put her arms around the man she held in the highest esteem. Coleman was boss in her eyes. Gently they came together.

Their lips touched and a kiss ensued as they held each other in the corner of the stairs. They lingered but for a moment, until the kiss was over.

"What will we do, my love?" she said. "When will we be free?"

Coleman said nothing as he spun her around and put his lips back on hers and together they spun a web of love that they could share but only when Brentford wasn't there.

Every day Coleman would visit his sister. She had been unwell for years. As a child she was always poorly but now after spending many years with doctors and spending virtually every penny they had on medication, it was decided an operation was needed. This would cure most if not all of her symptoms. Coleman knew he had to raise more funds to pay for the treatment.

After years of listening to his boss on how to buy shares or invest in commodities, Coleman had accrued a fair amount of money for himself and for his future with the maid. Now there was a more urgent reason to release this fund for his sister's operation. The only problem was that he did not really know how to turn all this paper into cold hard cash. There was another hitch though. He could not ask his boss to buy the shares and commodities because all of his investments were with Brentford's rival companies. He had hated his boss that much! He would sack us all, he thought.

Never the less, that evening, Coleman would ask his boss Brentford for a loan against his earnings, so his sister could get her operation quickly, then, when he could sell his paper wealth, he would pay it back ahead of time.

Brentford stormed through the front door as usual for him at the end of a long day. He threw his coat at Coleman. "Hang it up man and be quick about it" he scowled. I need my evening paper and a brandy before dinner. God man! It had better be ready". Before Coleman could answer Brentford had marched off towards his study.

Coleman calmly hung the coat on a hook in the hall and with as much poise as he could muster, he walked towards the study. It was another brow beaten evening for all the staff as Brentford went through the usual rhetoric about how lucky they all were and how good he was to them for keeping them on, in this day and age, with prices rising, unemployment rising and people continuing to moan about virtually everything. "It's a damn hard life" he added as Coleman poured him another large brandy. Coleman saw now that the warm room, a good meal and the best brandy was causing Brent to mellow, so he suggested Brentford move from the table to his favourite chair by the fire.

In the study, the maid had long since cleared up and she and cook could be heard working away in the kitchen washing the dishes.

"Good idea" said Brentford "Get away from that racket they are making".

Not long after, Brentford sat comfortably in his chair, Coleman flitted here and there, busy doing nothing really.

"Coleman" said Brentford. "What the hell are you doing man? You're making me dizzy with all this flurrying about".

"Sorry Sir" said Coleman "Just keeping busy until you are ready to retire".

Brentford stood up and made his way to the Atlas bar, he lifted the bottle of brandy and poured slowly. He didn't let

Coleman pour his drink this time. Coleman always poured it. Short, stupid man! He thought.

Brentford had a twinkle in his eye and what could only be called a smug look on his face.

"What's on your mind Coleman?" he said with an edge of scorn in his voice. "What trivial thing is wandering around that tiny mind of yours?" He walked back to his chair and sat down.

Coleman cleared his throat. It's now or never, he thought. Then in a servile manner he told Brentford about his sister and his hope for a loan, to put together the money needed. He didn't mention his investments. When he had finished, there was a moment of un-easiness between them.

Brentford stood and then he walked to the large patio window to look out at the huge garden.

"So" he said."It's come to this has it? This is what has been worrying you all this time and now by telling me, you would like me to be worrying too. Well I won't! I'm not going to worry, not about you or your sister and further to that there will be no loan either. I am not a bank or a loan club.

So do you think I am going to just give you money for something that I am not interested nor can I make a profit. I don't think so, Coleman, I don't think so. No Sir! It won't happen. You should have left things alone. Let things be, let nature take its path. All that treatment and all that money spent and no results. No cure eh! No cure. Maybe you should have let her go a long time ago, that might have been better for all. You would be free then eh! Free to continue your service without these side distractions and don't forget you tried to lay this burden of yours onto me. Well, no Coleman. It won't happen. I won't do it and nor will anyone else in this world. There are no saints, man. No saints here or out there.

Do what you have to do and be quick about it but leave me out of it and it better not interfere with your duties to me."

Then with such anger, he smashed his brandy glass on the table. The force of which shattered the crystal glass into a million pieces. He walked over to Coleman and stood right up to his face.

"Get that cleaned up. Now!" Then he turned and stormed out of the room and made his way upstairs. Coleman slowly cleaned up the mess but all the time trying to calm down his shaking body. He was seething with anger and he didn't like it.

Later Coleman stood facing the fire as the maid walked in. She knew what had happened. She had overheard it all from the hall. She slipped her arms around his waist and laid her head on his strong back. "I guess the answer was no then" she said. Coleman clasped her hands and sighed. "I just wish that I had never asked him. He will make my life hell from now on. He said that he was no bank or loan company and he would not be my sister's benefactor. The final insult was that I should have let her die a long time ago. What were his last words? Oh yes! There are no saints Coleman, there are no saints. He has to be the nastiest man on the planet.

They held each other for a while then the maid said "Why don't you talk to my brother? He has some knowledge of investing and shares. He seems to have done OK with it and he might be able to get the money you need." They walked towards the hall and turned towards the servants quarters arm in arm. When they reached the door, they stopped and kissed. "I think I will, said Coleman. I will talk to him. Anything is better than nothing. Thank you Darling." They kissed again. It was a deeper kiss this time. A kiss of love. He held her away. Looked at her beautiful young face and smiled. I am a very lucky man in one way, he thought. "I had better go check on him. You go to bed and I will see you in a few minutes."

Coleman entered Brentford's bedroom and as soon as he did. Brentford started again and for the next half an hour, he bawled Coleman out with curses and insults but eventually he got into bed and bade Coleman goodnight with a wave of his hand and a terse, "Get out!"

Coleman switched off the light, closed the door and stood for a while with his chin on his chest, then made his way downstairs to his room. The maid was waiting.

The following afternoon Coleman found refuge in his favourite bar. He sat thinking and planning his next move. Ten minutes later the door opened and in walked his maid and another man. They walked over to him and she introduced the man as her brother. Over the following hour or so they discussed a way forward. Each had a different plan but it soon became clear that they were all thinking along the same lines.

Over the next few days they put their final plan into action. Shares were sold, commodities moved or swapped, buying low and selling high. Picking off shares in Brentford's world. They would buy businesses in trouble, split them up and sell them off.

The money mounted, slowly but surely, they chipped away at Brentford's world. Over the weeks they were working, Brentford due to his arrogance and ignorance couldn't see the danger he was in, he thought he was untouchable. Then, the pressure began.

Phone calls from partners, asking what was going on. Why was his stock, being sold so cheaply and then sold on by the buyer at a huge profit. His directors queried why his sales were crashing. Business interests were waning and more seriously, banks were calling in loans, loans that had to be paid in full.

Now Brentford realised his world was crumbling. He could not get credit anywhere. He couldn't use his cards, no one would lend him money and his board of directors had deserted him and voted him out of the company. His mortgage company called in the balance on his large house.

Eventually it was re-possessed. He was bankrupt. He had lost everything. He spoke to his advisor and asked how all this had happened over such a short period of time. He wanted to know the details of what had actually happened. He learnt that a rival company, called C.M.C.S Inc, had made a concentrated attack on his world of finance.

That evening, he was silent as his driver took him home for a final night in his lost home. Tomorrow, the new owners move in. He said nothing as he passed Coleman, stood by the front door. He just walked to his study, opened the Atlas bar, picked up the brandy and poured out at least a triple.

"Coleman! Coleman!" he yelled "Get in here."

Coleman came in.

"Get the rest of the staff together Coleman, get them all here for a meeting right now."

In a few minutes they were all assembled before him. "Listen to me" he yelled "Listen to me all of you. I am broke and if I am broke, so are you." He laughed. "I am down to my last dime, in fact, I don't even have a dime." He laughed again. "Some rival company has seen to that" he said some company called C.M.C.S Inc. Everything has gone including this house and, if I am homeless, you are all homeless with me." He laughed again loudly. He poured what was left in the brandy bottle into his glass. "I 'm not alone in this" he said "because you are all in this with me and that means you are all losers."

He laughed again, this time with a gloating look on his face. "This, by the way, is nothing more than you all deserve. You were never really loyal to me. You gave me poor service and never appreciated all I did for you. I gave you a roof, good pay, security and all you ever gave back to me was grief, moans and groans. You Coleman, you were the worst, asking me for money, for your sister's treatment, trying to put pressure on me into helping you, when it was me that needed the help."

He eventually stopped ranting and looked up. He could see them all just standing and staring at him. Suddenly he noticed that there was an extra person in the room and she was in a wheelchair.

"Who the hell is this? He asked.

"This" said Coleman "is my sister. She has come to live here."

"Live here" Brentford raged "Live here. I don't think so. I don't own this house anymore so there is no way, my good man, no way." He sneered and laughed at them.

"So" said Coleman "You will be looking for work then?"

"Don't be stupid man, of course I will. Didn't you understand anything I just said?"

"Oh! I think so" said Coleman "I understand perfectly, I suppose you will need somewhere to stay as well?

"Yes, yes of bloody course I will. Have you not been listening man?"

"Oh! I've been listening" said Coleman "So I have a suggestion for you.

"Really?" said Brentford. "Yes really" said Coleman "you could actually stay and work here for me as butler and live in the staff quarters."

Brentford sat up in his seat with a look of horror on his face "What?"

"I'm not going to repeat myself" said Coleman "so for the last time do you want a job here or not?"

"Just who the hell do you think you are?" yelled Brentford. Coleman leant right over so they were face to face, just inches apart. "I will tell you who I am Brentford. I am the man that owns this house now and all you ever owned. I am the owner of your rival. C.M.C.S Inc: These people behind me are all shareholders in your world and the future in our new world."

"Have you got it yet Brentford, has it sunk in yet?" said Coleman. "No. Then let me explain and give you the cold hard facts. C.M.C.S Inc stands for Coleman, Maid, Cook and Sister. If you want that job Brentford, It starts at six thirty tomorrow morning and you will be looking after all of us. Or, of course, you could choose your other option and that is to leave now and live on the streets. Oh! Yes and by the way Brentford, there are no saints in this world, no sir. There are definitely, no saints.

THE OLD TELEGRAPH POLE.

The old Telegraph Pole stood away

A lonely cable in the wind did sway

Like a helpless arm hanging slack

Ten feet above the Railway Track.

Cut free from the speaker it held dear

Speaking times of trains that people would hear

But no voice now from the unknown face

A new system on the platforms

now in place.

The pole still stands so very tall

Fighting the elements one and all.

Between the platforms four and five

The cable swings as if alive.

If poles like this could only stay.

What happened then from day to day

The old steam trains would come and go

Through Ice and wind and even snow.

I'm going north an engine would scream

The whistle sounded through a plume of steam.

Black grey smoke from the funnel did rise

Clouds of smoke right up to the skies

There's a hiss and some squeals

As power is passed to the wheels

Spinning and sparking traction to find

Pictures of hell come into the mind

The old Telegraph Pole is lost in the fog

Not a tree now but an upright log.

No life it has and this is why

If it had eyes I know it would cry

It has nothing to do, just stand around

Between the tracks on Railway ground

The stoney land it has to bear

But there are no flowers growing there

But a purpose now

A perch to be

For a seagull landing place maybe.

Not always alone then, it has to be said

Even though the Pole is dead.

THE SEEDS OF DOUBT

Almost as in a dream, she sat in front of the mirror, slowly and deliberately pulling the comb, through her long blond hair. Her own natural blond hair, not bottle blond, she thought. Her blue eyes stared blankly forward not seeing. It must have been about ten minutes since Joan picked up the brush and sat down to get ready for the day but something held her attention. She didn't know what it was but it held her there.

When suddenly she broke free of her going nowhere thoughts, she lay down the brush, stood up from the bedroom stool and walked to the bed. She was quite tall and slim for her thirty seven years considering she'd had three children. As she bent forward to pick up her slippers, her breasts felt just a little heavy. She thought for a moment that they were possibly just a little big for her but it was just a passing thought. Sitting on the bed, she pulled on her slippers, stood up, pulled her dressing gown around her and tugged the belt a little tighter. Just another day, she thought, making her way down the stairs and into the kitchen.

The kitchen was neatly laid out, everything in its place, surfaces clean and dust free, as was the rest of her home. "I am lucky", she thought as she looked around, automatically filling the kettle and switching it on. Everything she did was as if on auto-routine as she moved around.

I've done this so many times, she thought to herself. Like other times before Joan dreamed of doing something just a bit different, something out of the ordinary not just routine.

Graham, her husband was nice, too nice sometimes. He has a good job, earns good money, has a company car and all the trimmings that go with his status, but boring. Yes boring. He can be Oh! so boring!

Take our holidays, she thought as she tilted her head to look at the ceiling. Same place for the past ten years. Rarely, do we go out or have friends or neighbours in for an evening meal with a glass of wine. Even when we do, it's the same old subjects to discuss, same old jokes. Eventually they turn it round to talk about work or something just as mundane.

"Oh! God, for something different" she said out loud.

By eleven thirty, she had all her routine tasks finished. She picked up a romantic novel she had started days earlier, moved across the living room floor to her chair by the window, openly staring down at the scenery, from their house, on the side of the hill. Nothing was moving even the wind had faded so the trees didn't move. She sat down and started to read.

The story was about a young farm girl who had fallen for; who she thought, was a wealthy merchant seaman, who in fact was a cunning smuggler. Never the less, the girl left the farm life and found herself on an island almost a prisoner, as she was stuck there while her smuggler went about his business at sea.

All very nice Joan thought. "The grass always looks greener," she said out loud. Then added "Serves her right," and emitted a short laugh. Joan carried on reading for a few more minutes before dropping the book in her lap and staring up to the ceiling as she had earlier.

By twelve thirty she was dressed and coming back down the stairs. Right! That's it. I've had enough she said to herself. She went into the hall and slipped on her coat and outdoor shoes, pulled the door open and in a purposeful stride, made her way to the gate at the bottom of the drive. The bus stop was just a short walk away and within minutes, a bus arrived and she boarded.

Twenty minutes later, she was in town gazing at the bright jewellers shop window. Very clever, she thought. Bright lights to make all the rings and things sparkle. That's what draws us in. Yes very clever. As she turned to go on her way, she took just a few seconds to watch a young couple looking at the engagement rings. Joan smiled as she passed by and silently wished the young couple, good luck. She crossed the road and headed for the Old Eagle Inn, where she knew Graham sometimes had his lunch.

As she entered, she was already looking round for him. She had never actually been there before. It was Graham's place, his little haven from the office, where he could get a bite to eat with his colleagues. He always moaned though, that he couldn't actually get away from work as he eventually ended up discussing work related matters with them. It was important that she spoke to him about the up and coming holiday and now was as good a time as any, as she was in the right frame of mind. She wanted a change from the usual holiday in Scotland, going with her sister and her children to visit old friends. Not this year. I've already started to make plans for a holiday abroad, she thought.

He wasn't there. She looked at her watch and realised that it was only one twenty five. Graham's lunch is from one thirty so he is still at work. She ordered a coffee and small cake then made her way to a corner booth by the rear wall. Each time the door opened she looked over the partition, each time she was disappointed. She had her speech all worked out, the

19

pros and cons and all the reasons. Turkey or Greece would be a better place for a holiday than Scotland again. After a few minutes, she realised the door had opened and shut quite a few times. She peeked over the partition for the tenth time and spotted Graham. She was about to rise; what she saw made her freeze, then drop back in her seat with a thud.

Graham was with another woman. She hadn't seen her face. "I must see her face" she thought. "Good God! Graham, not you. No, not you. You're not the type. No. You're steady Eddie, not a romancer at all. I've never seen you flirt, let alone have lunch with another woman. How long had this been going on? Does he really go to his book club on his Tuesday night out? Is that where he met her? Where did he meet her?" Her muddled thoughts were still buzzing around her head as she peeked over the partition once more. She caught a glimpse of the other woman. Then in horror she slumped back down on the seat and sat open mouthed for a few seconds until it hit her. "It's Claire. Claire is having lunch with Graham, in here. Here in his little haven. Claire, my sister Claire. She's divorced. Oh! No! She's divorced and Graham's in here with her. They must have planned it but when? He knows I never come here. Him and Claire! Oh! God. It can't be."

Joan knew that they had always got on well but never thought anything of it. Her mind was busy. Trying to remember the number of times she had seen them together. The parties, the weddings, even the holidays. They had always kissed Hello and Goodbye! Not passionately, just on the cheek. They have danced on one or two occasions. Graham had driven Claire home after she had babysat for them. Joan just couldn't imagine it. Those two, in his car or in bed together. A tight

20

feeling started to rise in her throat. Angry at his deception. angry that her sister was trying to take her man. She stood up and walked to the table they had been sat at. They were gone. It was only a moment ago she thought but an hour had passed while she was running the event through her head. Angry now, she pushed her way out of the door and onto the street. Her head was still spinning as she took the bus home.

Graham was late home. As he pulled up in the drive, she worked her way round the kitchen making dinner, still seething.

"Hello Dear" he said as he hung his coat, in the hall. He came through to the kitchen, put his arms around her and kissed her lightly on the neck. She tipped her head away slightly. Her reaction was cool. As she eased out of this arms and placed a dish of potatoes on the table.

"Are you OK Love? You look a little tired" said Graham. "Had a rough day at home" he said with a hint of laughter in his voice. Joan ignored him. Pulled out her chair and sat down. Graham sat opposite, just looking at her. Suddenly he said "Do you know. You look as beautiful today, as the day we met, just stunning."

"Thank you" she said whilst thinking to herself, how dare he say that, how could he mean that. He's just a cheat, a cheap cheat, a cheap lying cheat.

"I think" she said "It's time we had a talk Graham."

"Really, he said "what about?"

"Our holiday" said Joan.

"Our holiday?" said Graham, sounding slightly puzzled."Yes" said Joan "I want to go somewhere different this year, not Scotland and alone, just us two. No kids, no Claire, just us two.

"Wow" said Graham, a total look of surprise on his face. It was as if he had been caught out, thought Joan.

"Without Claire and the kids" Graham added. "Yes. Just us two" Joan replied with purpose.

"Well I can see the kids being OK with that but Claire, I think she will be disappointed" he said. "She doesn't have a lot of money and when we share, it helps to keep her costs down and anyway she's great company as well. Before he could finish, Joan repeated what she had already said. "Just us two Graham, just us two."

"OK" he answered. "Well, we can speak to her tonight."

"Tonight?" said Joan frowning

"Yes. I've invited her over tonight for a drink or two. I knew you wouldn't mind, she is your sister after all."

Yes, she is my nicely divorced sister. Devour a man little sister thought Joan.

"So when did you see Claire then, to ask her Graham?"

"Oh! I eh! I bumped into her today in the town.

"In town?" said Joan.

"During my lunch" said Graham" she had nothing on tonight so I asked her over."

Just then the door bell rang. "I'll get it" said Graham and made his way down the hallway to the front door.

Joan's thoughts were running wild. Bloody cheek! He has lunch with her, then, asks her over. What a nerve. Visions of them having steamy sex sessions, in Claire's bed, his office, his car, our bed. Oh no! Not our bed. God forbid.

"Hi Joan" said Claire as she entered the dining area.

"Hi" said Joan as they lightly touched cheeks.

Graham came through behind Claire wiping his mouth. Yes thought Joan, wiping off Claire's lipstick. You! You!

He moved to the wine rack." Red or white?" he asked.

"Red said Joan. "White said Claire.

"Oops! Difference of opinion there" said Graham. "One of each it is then girls."

The evening was passing as usual. Boring discussions about work, marriage divorce, the normal. Tonight though was slightly different. Joan had fully noticed that both Claire and Graham looked edgy and nervous. Joan thought she would push it a little and see how they reacted.

"What do you think of people you love, going behind your back and doing something you would never accept as normal? Not that I am saying either of you would go behind someone's back but it's in my book you see. He goes and does something. She finds out and well, now she has a decision to make. I know it's only a short story but?

"Joan" said Graham "What are you getting at?"

"It's in my book" said Joan.

"Joan" said Graham, a little louder "What are you going on about?"

"I saw you today" Joan blurted out

"What!" they both said together.

"In the pub, I was there" she said.

"In The Old Eagle you mean" said Graham.

"Yes" said Joan sheepishly.

"You were in the pub? Why didn't you come over" said Claire.

23

"You were together, having lunch" said Joan. Graham and Claire looked at each other. Graham said, "Joan. We have something to tell you."

Joan's throat went dry "What?" she said sharply.

"Claire and I did have lunch together today" said Graham "I didn't tell you because it was going to be a surprise from me to you."

"A surprise from you to me?" said Joan.

"Yes" said Graham "I asked Claire to lunch to ask her if she wouldn't mind if it was just me and you that went on holiday to Turkey and I thought, well, I just thought that…" Before he could finish Joan had reached over to put her finger over his lips. She stood up, leaned over, moved her finger and gently kissed him on the lips. Holding his face in her hands, a long passionate kiss followed.

Claire got up "I think it's time for me to go don't you. It looks like you two have other things on your mind. Anyway she said I've met a new friend, he asked me to go down to London for a week or two. He's a nice man, has a big house and his own yacht. Just my type Joan, if you know what I mean. If I like it down there I just might not come back." All this was said as she put her coat on and made her way to the door.

Graham and Joan did not hear the door close.

Yellow trumpets

Along the pathways, fields and lanes

Along the banks of grass

Nearby daffodils sway in the breeze

Yellow trumpets in unison weave

Strong stems bend and flow

The daffodils dance away we go

Like sentries at their posts they stand

Tall and proud and grand

Bright and clear they grow so fast

Sadly though it's not to last

Sad then that they soon will pass

Fade to brown then droop, dying

Stems will slowly weaken, dying

Heads will lie bleeding on the ground

Spring fades and summer comes round

Nature's clock is ticking away

No strength left for one last sway

Now just a memory our faithful hosts

Until next year when we will see

the return of this year's ghosts.

WILLIAM SEALY.

The whines of the incoming shells screamed overhead. Soldiers dived for cover, as the first ones smashed through the trees and brush. Pieces of wood in their thousands, some small like needles, some as big as spears and bigger, scattered through the air. If a man should dare and just put up his head, he would be dead in seconds. Some did and they paid the price with an ugly death. Death was ugly in any form, they all knew that, these men at the front.

Not William Sealy, he dug himself in so deep and narrow that there was no room for anyone else and if a shell should find the opening; that would be a million to one. Some men of his unit hoped that it would happen but Sealy was lucky, he always came through.

For the past three years William Sealy had gone from a normal young lad, to a killing machine. From a lad who was used to helping others around his home area, he now helped himself to the pickings of the war. Stealing from the living or the dead. The dead had a habit of giving up any gold teeth they had, some still warm. You'll get yours Sealy. He had been warned by many of his fellow men. You'll get yours. Sealy just laughed.

His hunting ground was the middle ground between the two fronts. The front was spread all over. No one man, friend or foe, knew exactly where it was, which made it hard to know if you were behind enemy lines or in front. This suited Sealy down to the ground, just like poaching at home. He knew how to be silent in any place, in deep brush or open field. As yet, he had never been caught.

The shelling continued for over two hours. The wood was decimated, with whole trees, blown to pieces, chunks of wood scattered for miles. Now, instead of an umbrella of branches and leaves, there were the corpses of both trees and men, strewn right through the valley. The sun burnt down now, with nothing to stop it.

Some men on both sides thought this made them more vulnerable, open to the spotters on the high ground. They could now pinpoint them and call in an artillery barrage, right on top of them. They could now see men walking or crawling, or even the wisp of smoke from a cigarette. All from the surrounding hills. Two hours ago the trees had given them some form of cover. Now the trees were all dead.

Sealy thought that this was right up his street. Now there was lots of ground cover and tonight he would make good use of it. Tonight he would be out and about, digging for gold amongst the corpses. The sun collapsed in the western sky. Night fell. The clouds were scattered and, every now and then, stars would show through and a ghostly light from the moon would move shadows across the graveyard of trees.

Sealy removed anything that rattled and anything he didn't need, blackened his face, then picked up his knife and dental pliers. Finally, wrapping his garrotte wire neatly and putting it in his top pocket. He crept forwards past the foxholes of his unit. "Get back in here, Sealy" whispered his sergeant. Sealy bellied his way across the uneven ground around torn trunks of trees and smashed branches. "Get lost" Sealy sneered. Seconds later Sealy was walking among the dead seeking the yellow gold that he had become a slave to. Every crack of a twig or the faintest rustle of leaves set his nerves on edge. Even the crack of a dead soldier's jaw as he removed a gold tooth made him cower silently for a few seconds. Then his nerve would return and he continued his grisly work.

For an hour or more, he made his way round the dead or dying. Those that weren't dead, he helped on their way with his knife or wire. Any good in him, had been evaporated from him. Now he did the devil's work for him and of course, he did it for the gold. Suddenly he caught sight of another figure ghosting its way along the ground and between the shattered tree trunks. Another hunter thought Sealy, wonder who he is? Silently he lowered himself towards the ground and crept away, back to his own area. The last thing he needed now was to meet someone, out here alone.

As he passed by the foxholes to his own pit he could hear the other men talking. Just whispers but as he passed by one hole, he heard his name. "That bloody Sealy will get his one day" he heard. "And when he does I will cheer" said another voice'

"He deserves a bloody death, that one" said another. " It's bad enough to die out here, let alone have someone mutilate your body afterwards."

Sealy dived towards the hole where he heard the voices, knife in hand, he threw himself in. "Who said that? Come on, who said that? You scum, if I find out who said that, I will watch where you fall and pay you a visit that night. It won't be just the gold ones I pull, I will pull the lot." He heard a click, then another, and realised he now had two rifles pointing right at him.

"Anymore talk like that Sealy and I will personally end your useless miserable life" said his sergeant. "Now get out and get in your own hole." Secretly, the sergeant feared him but he had to be strong for his men. He hoped a shell would make that million to one hit on Sealy's foxhole. Sealy sneered, then said "One day Sargy Boy, one day." He slid back out and snaked his way to his pit. A voice from the back of the foxhole muttered. "That man gives me the creeps."

The next day was much like the last three or four, pounding heads listening to the thunderous roar of guns and shells. Diving for cover one minute, up fighting the next. Hiding behind and among the friendly tanks going forward, dodging and running from the ones the foe put into battle in a counter attack. Back and forth, for days. Surviving, just surviving, that's what they were doing, that and killing and killing!

The earth died. The flowers died. The trees died. Nothing, including the men, would survive for long in this manmade hell. Even the will to live died in some of the men. Sealy still went about his devil's work. On one or two occasions he saw the other hunter but avoided him like the plague. A one to one fight with a man like himself was the last thing he wanted. God forbid, he thought.

Now he had a problem, one he needed to sort out for himself. "Just where do I hide my bounty? My future life" he whispered to himself. He thought it should be somewhere it would not be easy to find but somewhere that he could keep it on him. Then, if he was wounded and needed hospital treatment, some nurse or orderly could become rich in a minute.

He took a long draught of water from the melted snow in his pan. He carefully lowered his head below the edge of his foxhole. Pulled a poncho over his head, used his rifle to lift the poncho away from his face. He checked there were no gaps then lit one of the cigarettes he had taken from a body. As he drew the first puff in, he remembered the one thing a soldier must never be without. If you are naked and you have to run or if on the loo and you need to run, always take your gun. The soldiers best friend, soul mate, and wife. Always take your rifle no matter what. Slowly he stubbed out the last of his cigarette, eased himself to a more comfortable position. Picked up his rifle and stared at the butt end, turned it this way and that. He slid his knife from its sheath, slowly but surely he cut off the end making sure not to break it. This done, he turned to hollowing out the whole butt. Some hours later he was finished. The whole butt was hollow and he cut a wedge to jam the end piece in. The two small bags holding at least thirty teeth fitted inside just fine. He used some dirt and gun oil mixed together to cover the knife marks then spent a few minutes studying his handy work. He sat back a smug grin on his face, still room for another two bags in there, he thought. The he looked at the shavings and wood dust on the floor of his pit. Using his knife he cut away at the dirt wall and buried them out of sight. It was only then that he realised that he had missed a nights hunting.

The morning came with a deafening silence. There were no shells, no guns, no explosions, just whispering from the men close by. The wind blowing through the holes in the trees, made red hot by tracer bullets, sounded like an out of tune organ being played by a churchman who had maybe stayed too late at his local the night before. Even a small bird whistled away somewhere nearby. How in the hell has he survived, thought Sealy. He slipped his poncho around his shoulders, stooped and began zigzagging his way to the latrine pit some fifty yards back from his unit's position. He slipped off his poncho, hung it on a torn branch end and began relieving himself. Another soldier he didn't know approached the area, he spotted the poncho. "That's not army issue Pal" he said.

"None of your business" snapped Sealy. "Whoa, calm down man" said the other soldier "it's just that I might be interested in buying it. It being white you know. Give a little camouflage with all this snow." He said all this as he slowly lifted it from the branch.

Sealy had finished in the latrine and was stood right behind the other soldier. He quickly slipped his readied garrotte wire around the soldier's throat, he snarled and in his darkest threatening voice he said. "Hang it back up man or by God I will remove your head and send it to your mother."

The soldier, now with a blood line showing around his neck slowly replaced the poncho.

"Don't kill me! He begged.

Don't ever touch my stuff again, don't talk to me, don't even look at me" snarled Sealy. Then with one vicious move spun the man away, throwing him to the ground in a heap by the latrine pit.

Small beads of blood ran from the puncture holes on the man's neck. He stayed dead still until he realised Sealy had crept away. "God forbid, I ever meet that man again" said the soldier as he gently wiped away the blood from his wounds.

Sealy by this time had made his way back to his pit. Just as he lowered himself down, a new barrage began. Shells and mortar bombs landing right on top of his unit's position. Two men literally flew over the top of Sealy's hole. They were in pieces, legs and arms going in a different direction to the rest of their bodies. "Holy Mother, we are in for it now" screamed Sealy. Still screaming, he tucked himself down as low as he could go.' No one can hear me down here,' he thought.

Shrapnel, tree parts and body parts flew above but he dare not look up. For the next whole hour he trembled until the barrage was over. He and his unit readied themselves for the next onslaught.

This time the fighting was one way, backwards. Men were covered in blood, mud and gore. They were dripping with sweat from running fighting and killing. Arms and legs ached, heads pounded as their blood pressure mounted to brain blowing levels but still they fought on. Still they battled to keep ground. Stop the enemy breaking through but most of all they fought to survive.

The attack went on for most of the day and Sealy and his decimated unit found themselves in a wooded area virtually untouched by shell or mortar. Slowly but surely the battle abated and new foxholes were dug and a new winding front line made. Other than the odd sniper taking a pot shot at some vague target, which both sides had demanded should stop, the evening was quiet.

The enemy did not break through and hope held fast in men's minds that the following days wouldn't bring the death and carnage of this day.

Sealy geared himself up for a night jaunt among the trees and waste land beyond. His God was calling him. It was a damp and misty night, everything was wet. Sealy's skills in this weather would hold him in good stead. Just like home, he thought. An hour of searching, Sealy had done well, four gold ones. "The enemy must be rich" he whispered to himself. Something caught his eye to his right, it was his hunter friend and he had seen Sealy. Sealy snatched up his rifle and ran, head down to the wood. As he ran, he looked over to see his hunter friend doing the same thing. They entered the wood together about fifty yards apart and as the hunter dived for cover, he fired a shot at Sealy. Sealy fired back with three quick rounds before getting in amongst the trees. Sealy was lost. He didn't recognise this wood. He couldn't hear anyone or anything. Now other noises were alerting him to a bigger danger, cracks of twigs, crunching of leaves. He was here with another hunter just like him. Now they hunted each other, Sealy grinned, put himself in poacher manner and like a snake he wriggled his way through the underbrush.

Sealy saw him coming and opened fire, the hunter twisting and turning between the trees fired back. Both men, putting trees between them and the other gun. Each trying to catch the other out with skills learned from days past. Just what was this man's past? Thought Sealy. Ammunition gone, Sealy made himself a spear, short, like the Zulus. He was tired, sweating , cold as well, wet, all things he didn't need, in the battle he was in. They had clashed up close with empty rifles flashing and stabbing. Sealy had hooked the hunter's rifle away and smashed his over the back of the hunters head. The butt shattered. Had it been solid, it would have killed the hunter but it gave way and Sealy's hoard of gold scattered on the ground.

The hunter, who was out of ammo as well, used his skills in the same manner as Sealy, to arm himself. He was ready to fight to the death for what he knew Sealy had. The gold tooth he had seen glint in the moonlight that first night, not so long ago. He now knew about Sealy's booty on the forest floor.

The blow to his head did nothing more than enrage him and the spreading gold in the loose leaves gave him the will to fight on. Slowly but surely, as they circled each other and had thrown any weapon they had at each other, they were down to the knives and wires they both coveted.

Across a clearing, Sealy stood up and shouted "Come on my friend, come and meet your end. It was fate that you and I came together. Your death, my puny friend, leaves me with much more easy pickings."

The hunter stood up. "You mock me tooth stealer, pitiful small fry of a man, once I kill you, I will get the riches for myself. You will get yours, my unit tells me" said the hunter "but it's you who will get yours right now."

Slowly they circled, knives at the ready, then with all their fury threw each other into slashing, carving, fighting, each receiving wounds that would kill weaker men. Now they were wrapped in each other's arms desperately trying to kill each other. They fell, rolled, Sealy kicking, biting, doing everything he could to get the upper hand. The hunter did the same.

Suddenly Sealy found himself under his foe with his knife gone. The hunter's knife was nearing his chest. Weight and gravity slowly but surely pushed the hunter's knife deeper into Sealy's chest. He felt his heart and pulse racing as his breath slowly slipped away. "They said I would get mine" he said in a whisper. As his last breath left his body and his eyes began to close, the last thing he saw was a pair of dentist's pliers nearing his face.

THE RIVER WAITS

Cold runs the River Ness

Over slippery rocks

Below and far

Right through the heart of our town

Bubbles circle from salmon below

They draw the Angler near

Stressed rod bends with strain

The hook tears flesh and gum

The salmon pulls with the ebbing tide

Working together he breaks free.

The Angler stumbles

Then the dark soul of the river rises

Knees are buckled from the raging flow

The rod has long gone

Face down pounding the water

The Angler struggles ashore

Pulls out of the turmoil

The river relents and settles

Back to a steady flow

Or That's how it seems

To the Angler

'It wanted to take me', he mumbled

Those watching thank someone

For his life

The salmon below still lives bleeding

Life moves on

Along the River Ness

People turn away and shrug.

Whatever their thoughts are

The river waits and murmurs

Someone else will come.

THE GUARDIAN'S WARNING

Charlie Grey shot bolt upright in his bunk. The cabin was half lit by the early morning sun burning its way through the curtains. The four figures at the end of his bunk bathed in mist were slowly fading.

"Jesus!" Charlie whispered, "Not again. Who the hell are you?" he yelled. Then they were gone. He pulled the covers over his head and silently wished he hadn't woken up.

"Who are they?" he repeated in a whisper.

Time and time again this had happened over the past few weeks. Someone was calling his name in his sleep. He was dreaming he was in a huge cave on an island after being shipwrecked. He hears his name being called out but it's in his head, not out loud. Then, the four figures in the mist, just feet away, one beckoning with a long thin knuckled index finger. Their heads were much larger than usual, with large eyes. They shimmered, he thought, shimmered with a silvery satin effect.

The boat lurched in the increasing swell. From his cabin he could just hear the wind and he rolled further into his covers and closed his eyes.

The next thing he knew, he was thrown out of his bunk onto the cabin floor. The boat was rocking, dipping and spinning, water was pouring through the gap under the cabin door. He grabbed what he could of his clothes and put them on. Things were flying all over the place. More than once he banged his head, arm or leg. Shouting and swearing he eventually managed to get dressed. He slipped on his Mae West, he grabbed his boots and the chaos continued as he tried to put them on. He grabbed the latch and opened the door. The gangway was awash. More water was pouring down the steps up to the deck. No engine he thought where's the engine noise? No pump noise, just the slamming of the boat's hull against the crashing waves."Willie! He screamed "Willie! Where are you? Good God Willie what's happening? Andy, Phil, Where the hell are you?"

There were no answers as he made his way up the steps as best he could. The deck was level with the surface of the raging water. "Jesus! It's going under" he yelled out his friends names again and again. There was no reply. Suddenly he caught sight of a yellow vest some way off from the boat in the raging swell. Andy he thought that's Andy.
"Andy!" he yelled out, then again and again as the yellow vest spun further away, then it was gone.

He grabbed the last remaining float ring from the side of the roof of the boat, just as it tipped stern first, deeper into the crashing waves. Time and time again, he was under water, it poured into his mouth and out through his nose. Every piece of tissue in his sinus and throat stung. His eyes streamed with tears as sea water washed through them.

He gasped for breath but swallowed more water than air. The rain stung his face and it mingled with the salt and tears. He wiped his hand across his face as his head went under for the umpteenth time. He closed his eyes and slipped into unconsciousness.

A diamond of light crept into his eyes from under half closed lids. Water crept up and splashed his chin but his back was warm from the sun. He shook his head, dug his fingers into the sand and dragged himself up the beach away from the water.

Slowly, his senses returned and there was realisation that he had survived. God knows how but he had survived. Looking up, he could see the beach was lined with palm trees and tropical plants. Further inland there was a mountain but it was some miles off.

Once he had eventually got himself under the shade of the trees, he rolled into a ball and drifted off into an uneasy sleep. Suddenly he jerked awake and tried to sit up. It was dusk. As the sun slipped below the horizon stars started to appear by the million.

He heard his name. He spun himself around to see where it was coming from. It was in his head. He stopped turning and stared down the beach where there was a mist just above the water by some rocks. The four figures were there, all pointing inland towards the huge mountain. They glided across the beach towards the trees, taking the mist with them.

"Who are you?" He yelled the best he could. His throat was dry with thirst. Climbing to his feet, he stumbled to where the figures entered the trees. The wind in then trees and the noise he was making as he pushed his way through the undergrowth, were all he could hear. He stopped to listen, no animal noises, no birdsong, nothing. He pushed on. Then he suddenly stopped, tilted his head, water, trickling water. He turned towards the sound and crashed on. Within minutes he broke through into a clearing where there was a small pool. Oh! God he thought, thank you, thank you.

The cool clean water washed his throat and his face. He snorted water through his nose to clear it of sand. Putting his face right under the surface he opened his eyes and blinked a few times to wash them clear of salt. Moving forward he slid into the pool and started to swim around. He flung his head back and let out a full blooded scream of joy, then crawled out to the shore. Today's sun slipped away and darkness came as he tried to sleep.

His mind was busy trying to cover the events of the last few hours, the storm, the boat, his pals, and the beach where he woke up. Oh! My God' he thought. My old school chums, Willie, Andy and Phil. Did any of them survive? Am I left alone? It was meant to be a fishing trip, just an ordinary fishing trip. The weather must have changed while I was sleeping. They didn't wake me. Why didn't they wake me? Maybe there was no time. Maybe the storm came up too quickly or they didn't think it was going to be so bad. They should have called me or something.

Then into his bleary mind came the four figures. Who are they? What do they want with me? He dug deep into his subconscious and realised there wasn't four. It was only one figure, sort of three D effect, no, like a hologram only with depth. Yes that's it, there is only one figure but what does he want? Why is he picking on me? What's he trying to tell me? His head ached and he closed his eyes tighter to relieve the pain. The night stars burned brightly as he slept.

When morning came, he felt the pangs of hunger and put his hand to his throat and gave it a rub. Pulled his tongue around his mouth and realised how thirsty he was as well. He made his way to the pool and drank deeply. Looking round, he spotted a couple of coconuts below a tree. He picked one up. He had a puzzled look on his face, sort of how do I open it look? He smashed the coconut against the nearest tree, it shattered, spraying husk, shell and milk over him and the sand.

Quickly he grabbed at the pieces and sunk his teeth into the white flesh of the nut, getting a taste of the milk as he chewed hungrily

Feeling more lifelike now and a little fresher, he turned his eye on the mountain. Still eating his fare he took his first steps further inland. He hadn't gone far before he stopped to listen, again nothing but a slight rustle of leaves at the very top of the trees. Strange, no birds. It's warm though, yes it's very warm, he thought as he plodded on.

It took him just about an hour to reach the base of the mountain. There were no plants or trees growing on the lower slopes. No grass, just a grey dusty surface on hard rock. Looking up, he could see the feint grey of steam or smoke drifting up and out of what must be its crater. In just a few places, smoke appeared like the genie from the lamp, in spurts with a just audible hiss. He made his way round the base looking, just looking. He had no idea what he was looking for but he kept his eyes open for a sign of some sorts or something, anything out of the ordinary.

An hour or two passed and he saw nothing of any importance but just as he was giving up he spotted the roof of a hut in the trees below where he was standing. Sliding down the shale hill, under the trees and came to a stop by the side of a large rock. He picked himself up and headed for the hut. The nearer he got he could see more huts and people walking about. Natives. They were natives. He entered the clearing where the huts were. People stopped, they stared at him silently, as he walked further into the village. The people then moved aside as he walked through. One man who was taller than the others came from the large hut and walked toward him. They stopped facing each other.

Charlie put out his hand, he realised that it was shaking. However, offering to shake hands was an international hello, so it should be OK. The tall man took his hand and in broken English said "Welcome." He beckoned towards the big hut. Before long they were seated around a low table, so close to the floor that they were seated on cushions.

Fruit and drink came from various directions as the tall man, who Charlie now thought was the chief, tried communicating in all sorts of verbal and sign methods. Eventually Charlie had told and relived his tale of how he got there. The chief nodded often as if understanding everything being said. Suddenly there was a loud grumble and a violent shaking of the earth. The volcano was letting off steam. Charlie stood up and walked to the door and looked up to the ever increasing steam and smoke coming from the crater. He said quietly

"That's going to blow" then out loud, he said it again. "That bloody thing is going to blow." He turned quickly to the chief. "You have to leave. You and your people have to get off this island, all of you."

The chief shrugged his shoulders, not understanding. Charlie grabbed a stick. He quickly drew a picture of the volcano with an outline of the island. Round the outside he drew waves for the sea then he stood up, threw his arms in the air and shouted out loud "Boom! Boom!" and other noises that he thought would give the impression of exploding flame and lava. Grabbing the stick he drew what he thought looked like lava pouring down the side of the smouldering hillside. He grabbed a tree and indicated it falling over again using noises

41

to emphasise his meaning. The chief waved his hands and repeated. "Yes. Yes. Yes I see. Yes I see. What should we do?"

"Leave" said Charlie "You must leave now. Get all your boats, tie them together. Get food and water and warm clothing. Make a large raft. Make a sail or two. Do everything now and quickly."

The chief called his people together. Gave them orders and soon they had everything ready, as Charlie had suggested. The island shook, giant fingers of flame leapt out of the volcano's mouth of hell. Boiling hot stones cascaded down from the heavens as Charlie watched the boats and rafts float away. He turned, there was a misty figure pointing out to sea. Just then, a huge rock hit him on the head and as he slipped into the abyss of unconsciousness, he murmured "I've left it too late. I've left it too late."

Charlie threw himself upright in his bed, sweat pouring from all over his body. "Good God! What's going on!" he said out loud. He climbed out of his bed and staggered to the window looking down the harbour. He searched for his pal's boat, not seeing it, he opened the window, then spotting the port officer, he yelled out to him. "Where's our boat? Where are the lads? Have you seen them?"

The port officer looked up, he shouted out. "They left earlier. You were still asleep, so they went without you."

"Jesus!" said Charlie "Get them on the port radio. Get them back. There's danger out there. Get them back." The port officer laughed. "There's always danger out there, Charlie" he said.

"No! I mean real danger. Like a tidal wave. Yes, that's it. A tidal wave. Put out a warning."

"What?" shouted the port officer. "What are you talking about?"

"It's a volcanic island" Charlie screamed out. "It's going to erupt and sink causing a tidal wave. You have to get them back and warn everyone." Charlie then slumped back into his bed.

After a while he got dressed, walked over to the TV set and pushed the control box for the news channel. As he sat in his chair, the pictures came clear. Pictures of a volcanic island erupting, belching out fire and brimstones from the depths of hell. As the pictures moved to somewhere that had been wiped out by a huge wave and then to an un-affected beach where lots of small rafts and boats were lined up, lots of people in native clothing were partying. A tall man came forward to speak. It was the chief." We were so grateful" the chief said, "so grateful to our guardian from the mist. He warned us that this was going to happen. He drew the events in the dust and screamed and sang out his warning. So we left. He was still standing on the beach as we left. The pictures he drew were the same as on the cave walls that our guardian had drawn years before. This was his forecast for these events. Then he came back to save us."

Charlie sat open mouthed as he listened. Just then a shout from outside got his attention. He ran to the window and threw it open. There, down below were his pals Willie, Andy and Phil. "God man! Where have you been? You went without me."

"We are coming up Charlie. Put the kettle on."

In just a few seconds his pals came through the door. They threw their arms around him. "Charlie my boy, we are safe, thanks to you."

"What are talking about?" Charlie asked.

"It was you Charlie. You gave us a real scare. You were suffering with some sort of fever. We took it in turns to look after you and every day you kept telling us about this volcano thing for about two weeks. At first, we all took it lightly but then, we heard something over the radio about a report from a pilot of a passenger plane that he had flown over an island that appeared on fire. As far as we know it wasn't on any maps and no one knew it was there. Well. We do now."

"So where did you go in the boat then" asked Charlie.

"Well" said Andy "We took your warning to heart and along with all the other owners, we moved our boats to a safe harbour further round the coast.

"What about the tidal wave?" asked Charlie.

"It was huge" answered Andy "but it went the other way. Some places were wrecked but because of you we had time to tell the world what was going to happen. So many people were saved. It hit here but damage was light. It could have been worse. It would have been much worse for us though.

Had it not been for you, coming to warn us, out at sea. That's why we came home early."

"I came to warn you?" said Charlie How did I do that when I was here ill?

"Well said Phil "you came to us alright, like a mist. A sort of hologram. You made it clear that we had to return home and we did. Aye! Just like the appearance of the man before those natives from the island. That was you too Charlie, wasn't it?"

After a bleary few minutes Charlie fell back onto his bed. "He's whacked" said Willie "Come on, leave him be. Let's get a dram. Come on. Praise God, we are alright."

"I'm not sure about God" said Andy "Our pal Charlie played some part in this."

Charlie closed his eyes as they left. It was me he thought, me Charlie! It was me. Holy Mother, I was the guardian. It was me!

IN THE DARK

It's a long, long drag from morning till night

Though I won't see it

The sun will grow

Yellow and bright

Shadows will dance on the grass

Through trees blowing in the breeze

I still won't see it

A thundering train will look

Like its flying

Right through our Glen

Crystal lights will flash

On the loch nearby

I will not see it

People will scurry hither and thither

Children will shout and scream when playing

I want see or hear them.

I live in the dark

I work in the dark

I sleep in the dark

I long for a break on a warm summer's day.

So I might see the colours

Hear the songs

And whistle a tune

Hold my childrens hands of white

Mine are black

I wish so that I could look upon

My beautiful wife in sunlight

Not by the lamp in our room

Why?

Because I live in the dark

I work in the dark

I sleep in the dark

I live in a world of flickering orange light

There are ghostly figures with no faces

I don't see them whole

Just the whites of their eyes

I am a miner

It's a working man I am

And only when I die

Will I be in the light.

THE PAGE AND THE KING

The King stood, then strode to the window, looked out upon his land. Minutes passed, and then he turned back to his throne. On sitting, he called "Come kneel Page, so I may rest my feet. Weary they are from standing."

The Page knelt then before him, where upon he placed his feet firmly to the Page's back.

A groan uttered from the Page. "How is it, my king, and that your feet weigh that of a new born baby each, upon me?"

"Tis your purpose" said the King "to carry the weight so I don't have to."

"Would not my King, look to a stool "said the Page.

"A stool?" said the King "a stool?"

"Yes, you could look to a stool" said the Page.

"But then you would have no purpose. You Page, would have no place in my castle. On the outside you would live, to find your own way."

"Not so" said the Page "could I not sit on the end of the stool, your feet on the other, then I could impart my advice from a level of the goings on in your land."

The King smiled at his guile, then called aloud "Carpenter, come forth."
He came. "Look upon this sight" the King said. "Take you paper and charcoal. Measure and draw what you see. Make me a stool likened to my Page."

"My Lord" said the Page "Would not you consider but two stools, that way I could sit myself beside you and together, hope to find the glory for your lands."

"So, my Page would look to be my guide, my mentor and saviour of my land" said the King. "So shall it be, Carpenter, make you two stools."

To the Page he then said "Pour me wine and fetch bread."

The Page broke the bread and poured the wine, then served it to the King. Returned to the table, where upon he broke more bread, poured more wine and satiated his own hunger and thirst.

The King watched, Agog!

But one day passed, the carpenter returned. He placed to the floor, two stools. Both made to look like the Page. "For you my King" he said. He bowed and retreated from the room.

The Page smiled in his head, not to carry the King's feet again but to sit beside him in reverence. Not bad for a Page, he thought.

The King then spoke "Come forth to me my wife and son." Where upon he placed the stools, one to each side of his throne. They came to him. "Sit you both down beside me and you Page, kneel before me so I might rest my feet upon you."

"My King" said the Page "I thought I might do so much more for you then just rest your feet."

"You will, my loyal Page. From this day forth, you will take the weight of my royal family's feet whence they should call. Threefold shall your duties be for your King, more hours you will take upon you for your King sees you as staff, on which we shall rest so we be fresh whilst we plan our future."

The Page sighed, his plans in shreds.

"That if you should think to look upon your King as equal, so you will find the task daunting."

The moral of this story is that even if you have such a dream, you should not speak of it or you may get your just rewards.

When I was a lad.

When I was a lad

I splashed in puddles in my shoes

They filled up with water and soaked my socks

My mum caught me by the lobe of my ear

She had a way to bring my eye to a tear.

When I was a lad

I would scrump apples from the orchard nearby

It was owned by farmer Kibble

My mum caught me by the lobe of my ear

She knew how to bring my eye to a tear.

When I was a lad

I broke the window next door

I denied it till I was blue in the face

My mum caught me by the lobe of my ear

She could always bring my eye to a tear.

When I was a lad I stole a fag from my dad

He caught me smoking it down by the shed

He took off his belt

And wrapped it right round my bum

He could bring both my eyes to a tear.

Now I'm grown up

I'm a man so to say

I think of my parents every passing day

I'm not being punished

I've got nothing to fear

Its only my memories that bring my eyes to a tear.

MR. "EASY"

Jim Penn closed the door of his new car and stood back to see it from the side. He took a good look through the window to view what other people would see if they looked in. Nice he thought, very nice.

He opened the rear door and picked up a suit case and travel bag he loaded earlier at the air port. He had a contented look on his face as he pressed the lock button on the cars key. The click , click of the doors locking system sounded as he walked off towards his own front door. The last couple of days have been real easy he thought as he put the house key in the door lock. He opened the door and stepped in, there were a few letters lying on the floor, he gently kicked them aside, pushed the door open further to squeeze in with his luggage.

Then using his foot he pushed backwards to shut the door. He stood for a moment while he gathered his senses, put the luggage down in the hallway, bent down to scoop up the mail and walked down the hall to the cupboard by the kitchen door. He opened it, reached inside to pull up the mains switch to house, a light came on in the hall and another in the kitchen ahead, he opened the kitchen door and walked in.

It was just as it was a few days ago. The fridge and freezer doors were still slightly ajar as he had left them. They don't smell that way he heard his mother say in his head. Nice and fresh he thought , nice and fresh ,easy.

He turned and went back down the hall, picked up the

bag and went back to the kitchen, placed the bag on the work unit and began to empty its contents, cheese, milk, margarine, a few micro meals, bread, two or three jars of various jams and two jars of olives. He loved olives. Slowly but surely he worked his way to the bottom of the bag putting the various items away in the units as he went. Job done he turned to walk away. He stopped and let out a sigh as he realised he hadn't brought any coffee or tea bags, oh well I get some tomorrow. Easy, he thought.

No tea for me in the morning he muttered. He suddenly felt weary from the last few days escapades, time for a lay down he said out loud and made his way to his bedroom back down the hall.

The bed was already made. He slipped off his shoes, sat on the side of the bed before swinging his legs up and at the same time dropped his head onto the soft pillow. He very soon dropped off to a very uneasy sleep, easy he thought.

It was dark when he woke up and a sense of unease came over him again as he remembered what he had been doing over the last few days.

The flight had gone to plan. in fact the whole scenario had worked out real easy so what the hell am I worried about he thought.

I was given the job in exactly the same way as all the others, a phone call to my unregistered number, details left in a box at a station of my choice, picked by a courier and delivered to a private address in a building of condemned flats. easy.

Every thing he needed was in the envelope, photos, addresses , flight tickets organised. He had then sat down to read a few details of his task which was also in the envelope. Easy. It was easy, he said, everything went according to plan, nothing went wrong.

Jim made his way to the hall and picked up his case and took it to the kitchen. He laid it gently on the work top and placed his thumbs on the latches and gave them a flick. The locks clicked open and he raised the lid. Inside there was an assortment of clothing and one pair of shoes he lifted them all out and placed them on the unit top. He ran his fingers around the inside edges of the case found the secret latch he was looking for and pushed it down. The bottom of the case moved and one edge opened. He gently lifted it , it was a little heavy, it was made of lead, a very thin sheet that was the lid of a box that made up the bottom of the box, the whole box was made of lead ,x-ray proof but still very light.

Two small handmade pistols lay in the box, they were made from wood and plastic, no metal involved. Half a dozen home- made bullets laid in a specially made clip under one of the Pistols. Another clip was under the second gun but this one was empty. Once again he had a feeling of unease, I can't think why he thought everything went beautifully - easy peasy.

Jim put the case back together walked to the cupboard in the hall and placed the case on the floor inside. He went back to the kitchen sorted out all the clothes for washing and put them in the machine, as he pressed the button to start it he got a small shock of electricity through his finger. He stood back in shock and looked at the machine with a frown on his forehead.

"What the hell!" he said out loud , then he spotted a thin wire coming from behind the machine up to the button panel, it was almost invisible. "Jesus what the hell is that?" He thought.

He quickly switched off the machine at the plug and pulled it out from its recess, the wire was attached to a motor. Tthat's when it hit him, it had been done deliberately. Who the hell? How? Why? His head was a mass of mixed messages. He sat down with sweat running from his brow. He grabbed some kitchen roll and wiped his face. "Someone wants me dead" he thought, "or do they, they must have known it wouldn't kill him, just scare him, yes - just scare him but why?

He looked around the kitchen at the other electric items in there, the kettle, the fridge- freezer the coffee machine He checked them all. He found nothing untoward Now he was worried. He slowly made his way round his home looking for other little surprises he may have been left.

One small item by his lamp in his bedroom caught his eye, no bigger than a match head pinned to the shade a small antennae thin as a hair poked out from the top, the smallest listening device he had ever seen. it was only then he realised he was still sweating. Beads of sweat were trickling down the side of his face and tickling his cheek. "Good God man get a grip" he thought to himself, I don't sweat ,I just don't sweat, no matter what.

He sat down in the bedside chair, slumped would have been a better description, then grabbed a tissue and wiped his fac. He shut his eyes and tried to put it all together. The last job, it must have been something to do with my last job, revenge, someone wants revenge someone wants payback. that's it, that's it ,easy someone found out what he had done and wants revenge, the question is who?, yes who?, the client? clearing up loose ends?. Another man like him? looking to get rid of competition . A victim's friend or relative?, getting their own back, no that last one is impossible no one in that group knows him, that was for sure.

Competition could that be it? No, he thought I don't know any other man like me, so how would they know me, unless of course my client told them about me but then the client would be removing a first class man like me and I have always served him well. His sub Consciousness kicked in and now he was having a two way conversation with himself. Yes that would make sense, I know enough about my client maybe that's what this is about, yes that's it. He knows I know and has hired a man like me to get rid of me. Easy.

It was night when he opened his eyes. He ached. His head was feeling thick. He made his way to the kitchen, got a glass and turned the tap on for cold water, it ran hot. He slammed the glass down on the draining board ,stood back and just stood looking. Then he knelt and opened the unit door below the sink. There was clear evidence that someone else had definitely been in his home when he was away. The hot and cold supply pipes had been swapped over but why? This kind of thing wouldn't kill him, just annoy him more and get him angry, but I don't get angry, I always stay calm no matter what. If you get angry you lose concentration so I am always in control. Easy.

He swapped the pipes back over, poured his water, added some ice from the freezer and sat on a kitchen stool. In his head now whirled the plans he was concocting on just what to do, how to clear this matter up. First thing in the morning he must contact his client and do some fishing, try to get a clue if he was involved. Then make some enquiries to see if any of his associates know of any new men of his talent in the neighbourhood. He stood up and headed for the kitchen vent by the back door, it was set in the brickwork above the door frame. He fumbled in his pocket to find his keys, selected the one he needed and put it in the vent lock and opened it, swung open the vent door and put his hand in, placed his fingers around the gun he had hid there and gently pulled it out. he glanced over it to check it out, then removed the magazine, it was loaded, he slipped the safety catch on and put the gun in his waist band. almost automatically he side stepped to the window and took a sneak look out to his rear garden, nothing was moving, he moved from side to side looking both ways as far as he could. He knew if any one came near his fence the two large security lights would be triggered and flood the rear garden with blinding light, it had happened before when kids kicked a ball over his fence, he was watching television when a small red light which flashed on a warning panel by the tv, came on. He had rushed to his kitchen, opened his back door and screamed at them to clear off. Yes he thought, but that was months ago. Suddenly he was slammed back into defence mode remembering the situation he was in and strode through the house to the front room window. Carefully he pulled the curtain but only just enough to see out. To most people the street would have looked as normal but his senses were on full alert right now and the medium sized van parked a few houses away immediately grabbed his attention. As did the man stood beside it having a cigarette, he was looking up and down the street as if he was looking for someone.

Jim moved to the other side of the window and peeked out. There were two workmen putting up a small tent over a man hole just the other side of the zebra crossing about twenty yards down the road, one light on the crossing was not flashing. Maybe they are genuine workers and are repairing the light he thought. Damn flashing lights. He hated them and had often complained to the council about putting some kind of barrier board on the path side to block the light shining on the houses nearby but his complaints went unheard or, at least, were not dealt with.

Suddenly he caught a glimpse of movement on a roof above the shop on the other side of the road, some hundred yards away. Staring and searching with his eyes through the early morning light he tried to see the man again but he couldn't. Ideal spot for a sniper up there, he thought and tried once more to see the man. He couldn't. As he turned to move away from the window he caught a view of the park wall, further down the other way of the road and turned his head to look more carefully. The light was improving so he could see a lot further. He blinked and stared for a second and a short gasp left his throat as he spotted the old man sitting on a fold up stool next to some paintings leaning against the wall, a hat was by his feet and the old man had his chin resting on top of a walking cane. Now who in hell is he Jim said out loud, is that a cane or some sort of gun he thought.

A quick glance at the clock told him that it was 6.45 am. He turned back to the window and watched the milkman walk to his neighbours door step and place two bottles down. As the milkman turned around to return back down the path he looked straight at Jim Penn just behind his curtain. Jim snapped back. He didn't recognise the milkman, another stranger in his road. Either he was new or standing in for the regular man or maybe someone more sinister. He realised his neighbour never had two pints , never, I wonder if he is the one I should be wary of? Why did he leave two pints next door, when they normally have one?

Jim quickly walked to his front door and gently opened it to see where the milkman had gone but he was out of sight and his float was gone. Jim never had his milk delivered. If he had to sneak off somewhere, he didn't want anyone to know and milk building up on his door step was a dead giveaway for an empty house, even cancelling it could give him away.

Jim knew he couldn't stay indoors all day. He had things to do, bills to pay and that meant he had to go out sometime. He also knew he couldn't carry his pistol around the streets, It's different if you're hunting a mark, you're hiding ,so no one can see you. Even the police don't see me he said, Easy. The milkman had clearly shown his face, why would he do that if he were a professional? Unless of course he was an egotist, over confident and a very cocky man who would do this just to put Jim on edge.

Well, he thought, if anything is going to happen it will have to be when he stepped out of his front door. That is when, if any time, for him to be taken out or whatever was going to happen

I wonder who, what or how it will happen, he went round his house collecting his shoes and clothes, slipped his shoes and jacket on, walked to his front door, opened it and stepped out...   **READ ON**

THAT'S IT READER

I HAVE A NUMBER OF OPTIONS IN MY HEAD FOR AN ENDING
TO THIS SHORT STORY - ALL WITH A TWIST OF SUGAR OR
LEMON, SO WHAT'S YOURS? HOW WOULD YOU FINISH IT?
WILL YOU KILL HIM? DOES HE LIVE? IS IT ALL FALSE, ITS UP
TO YOU.

PLEASE SEND ALL YOUR ENDINGS TO JOHN GREENE
(LOWBERRY) C/O. FOR THE RIGHT
REASONS PUBLISHERS, GRANT STREET, INVERNESS, IV3 8BS.

This is not a prize winning competition it's just for fun.
The first ten entries will receive a complimentary, poetry book
with music c.d. if postal address is supplied.

WORKING IN THE SUMMER.

The morning sun burns through the glass roof

Sweat pours from my brow

It soaks my collar and back

My shirt does not breathe

My trousers heavy like canvass

Stick to my legs

I cannot bend

My body's a furnace

 it's only nine o'clock

The sun rises

the temperature rises

My skin leaks the more

I drink to sate my thirst

The water comes straight back out

Like a stream through my pours

Oh for a thin cotton shirt

Oh for trousers that breathe

I pray for boots that are soft

Easy to wear and light to lift

The sun rises the heat rises

I feel a breeze and hope

Hope for a cloud for shadow

No remorse the heat continues burning

At last the end of my shift

I can move on

Go home to cool

I'm in the shower at home

Still sweating but rid

Rid of my boots and uniform

The coolness of night

It's a blessing lying

In cool clean sheets

But I dream

I dream the dread of the morning sun

The dread of working in the summer

Under a glass roof

In a uniform made for the winter.

THE BIG BLUE BUS

Some time ago in the south of Scotland, some men were working hard to build a big bus. When it was nearly finished, the bus went to the paint shop for his new coat and they sprayed him a beautiful blue. Some men were talking and one of them said, "He looks great", then held his arms open wide and said out loud, "The Big Blue Bus," From that day onwards, that was his name.

The foreman said to his men that he thought the Big Blue Bus was magic. "Why?" one of them asked. "I thought I heard him say thank you" said the foreman "thank you for my new coat."

The men laughed and patted him on the back and went for tea. The foreman looked at the Big Blue Bus and said "You did, I'm sure you did." Then he turned to walk away. The Big Blue Bus winked his right headlight, giggled to himself and let out a quiet 'Toot, toot, toot.'

The following day a man came to see the Big Blue Bus and fell in love with him, almost at once, so much so that he decided he would buy him and take him home to Inverness at the top of Loch Ness where he lived. On the long journey to Inverness the Big Blue Bus decided he would surprise his new owner and suddenly he said "Hello John, thank you for buying me. I won't let you down, ever, thank you."

Just for a second John panicked and let go of the steering wheel. He grabbed it back and got control again. "What?" said John "What did you say? Did you speak? No it's not possible. I knew you were special but speaking, that's impossible. Buses can't speak."

"I can" said the Big Blue Bus "I don't know why but I can."

"My word! Oh! My word" said John "how wonderful." They both laughed all the way to Inverness. They chatted like old friends. In his excitement John pressed the horn and a loud toot, toot, toot came from the front of the Big Blue Bus. "What a great sound" said John and pressed the horn again and again, toot, toot, toot,---- toot, toot, toot.

The Big Blue Bus saw the view from the top of the hill as they headed down towards the town. "What a view" he whispered. "Aye" said John. The Kessock bridge over the Moray Firth, then beyond over the Black Isle and northwards.

They arrived at the garage where he was to be kept; it was clean, shiny with bright lights. "Wow" said the Big Blue Bus," toot, toot, toot, what a place." A special bay had been painted on the floor for him and John parked him there for the night. "Goodnight" said John. "Goodnight" said the Big Blue Bus.

The Big Blue Bus settled into his new home and very quickly began to carry passengers all round Scotland on tours or holidays. He really did enjoy himself and often let out his toot, toot, toot. People laughed as they knew when they heard that, the Big Blue Bus was not too far away.

He made some new friends: Horace the sports car, Morton the motorbike, Travis the train and Larry the lorry. There were a few others, one being Cybil the cycle, "ding, ding, ding" went her bell," ding, ding, ding". The Big Blue Bus always gave her a lot of room when he saw her as she and her rider were very vulnerable. If he was to let out a loud toot, toot,

toot, it may cause them to fall, so he always went "toot, toot, toot", very softly when he was near them.

One day when the Big Blue Bus was parked in the bus station, he heard a loud "beep, beep, beep" from behind him. He looked in his mirror and saw Horace the sports car and gave him a toot, toot, toot. "Hello Big Blue Bus, "said Horace "where are you going today?"

"Hello Horace" said the Big Blue Bus "I'm on tour today, I'm taking some folk on a round trip from Inverness, down Loch Ness to Drumnadrochit to see Urquhart Castle then back up to Beauly via Cannich then onwards to Achnasheen, Kinlochchewe and to Gairloch on the A 382 road."

Wow!" said Horace "you really know your way about. I wish I did. Then I could go as well. I've never really been out of Inverness since my owner Peter bought me."

"That's sad" said the Big Blue Bus "but I may be able to help you."

"How" said Horace.

"Well, I could ask John to speak to Peter and ask him to let you follow me."

"Do you think he would?" said Horace.

"We will see" said the Big Blue Bus. A little later he told John about Horace. John nodded and said "Leave it to me. I'll do what I can."

A short time later John and Peter returned "Right" said John "'let's get ready to go."

"Is Horace coming too?" asked the Big Blue bus. "Yes "said John "no problem."

"Yippee!" said the Big Blue Bus and let out a roaring, "toot, toot, toot."

"Beep, beep, beep, honked Horace "Hooray". Beep, beep, beep.

The passengers climbed on board and off they went out of the bus station and into the town. The Big Blue Bus led the way, followed closely by Horace as they headed out of town to the A82 that led to Loch Ness. Both of them were very excited and quite often you could hear a loud "toot, toot, toot" and a "beep, beep, beep" as they made their way down the road. It was raining at Urquhart Castle so they only stayed for an hour but everyone had a good time there and at the exhibition and shops in Drumnadrochit. The trip westward to Gairloch was wonderful, the sun was now shining and all the passengers were laughing and Horace and the Big Blue Bus were singing along with a toot, toot, toot and a tuneful beep, beep, beep. When they parked at Gairloch the Big Blue Bus giggled to himself when he saw Horace parked near the sea with his soft top down, head lamps closed and a grin on his front grill. "Ha! Ha!" and "toot, toot, toot" went the Big Blue Bus. Horace opened one headlamp and looked at him, his grin grew wider and he answered with a loud "beep, beep, beep." They were having a great time.

The trip back to Inverness meant a visit to Inverewe Gardens near Poole. John drove the Big Blue Bus into the car park and there was Larry the lorry with a load of plants and trees for the gardens. Larry saw them too and in his excitement the great trumpet horn on his cab roared out a long b---ar--p, b---ar--p, b---ar—p.

Everyone was looking round to see where the noise was coming from and when they least expected it, Horace and the

Big Blue Bus answered with a chorus of "beep, beep, beep", "toot, toot, toot", "beep, beep"," toot, toot".

John, Peter and Kim, Larry's driver, laughed and laughed for they knew what was going on. As evening came they reached Inverness and the passengers collected their belongings and as they left the Big Blue Bus they all thanked John for a great day.

Peter shook hands with John, jumped into Horace and drove away. Horace's horn beep, beep, beeped and faded in to the distance.

John parked the Big Blue Bus in his space in the garage, patted him on the radiator, said goodnight and went home.

What a day thought the Big Blue Bus, what a day and as his tired headlights were closing there was a faint toot, toot, toot.

He drifted off to sleep dreaming of what great adventure he could be facing tomorrow and hoped it would be as good as today.

'Toot, toot, toooot!'

The Big Blue Bus awoke; the sun was shining through the window at the front of the garage. He gave a shiver and a shake to wake himself up "toot, toot, toot" what a beautiful morning.

The door opened and John appeared. "Good morning John" said the Big Blue Bus.

"Good morning" said John "did you have a good rest last night? I hope you did" said John "we have a long way to go today. John checked the Big Blue Bus for his water and oil then all his lights and tyres. "Well, my friend, you're fit to go."

"Yippee! Toot, toot, toot", went the Big Blue Bus. "Where are we going today?" he asked

"Oh! Er! Somewhere secret today" said John. "It's a mystery tour, so to speak. I'll tell you as we go along."

"Is Horace coming today?" asked the Big Blue Bus. "He might be" said John with a wry smile.

Just then there was a "ding, ding, ding", outside the door. Cybil and her rider had arrived. "Toot, toot, toot "said the Big Blue Bus. "Ding, ding, ding" went Cybil. "Hello. Good morning! What a beautiful day" said Cybil. "It is" said the Big Blue Bus.

"Where are you going today? Asked Cybil. "I see you are ready to go for a run. Is it South or East? Do you know yet?" "No" said the Big Blue bus "today is a bit of a mystery at the moment. John knows where but he is not telling."

"Wow!" said Cybil "I wonder if I could come to find out, where it is you are going. I could fit on your cycle rack near the front" said Cybil.

"Don't worry" said the Big Blue bus "I can talk to John, maybe he can ask your rider to come along."

The deed was done. John spoke to Cybil's rider, her name was Karen and it was very clear that she and john were very good friends. "Oh! Yes! Said Cybil and she rang her bell, ding, ding, ding; ding, ding, ding. Karen fitted Cybil to the rack and John started up the Big Blue Bus's engine. It roared into life with a brum, brum, brum, brum, brum, brum.
John and Karen smiled at each other as the Big Blue Bus roared out with a toot, toot, toot.
A few moments later they arrived at the bus station, hundreds of people were wandering around.

"I think some of them are lost" said the Big Blue Bus to John. "I think you are right" said John never mind, I can see our customers just over there, so come on, let's go and pick them up."

There was a real mixture of people, some from France, Germany, America, and Australia. In fact, from all over the world, even from Japan and China.

When everyone was settled on board, off they went, out of the bus station. "Hoorah!" went the Big Blue Bus, then he and Cybil joined together to play a tune for the trip.

'Toot, toot, toot, a ding, ding, ding; a ding, ding, ding and a toot, toot, toot!'

John turned the Big Blue Bus out of the garage to the left and onto the main road out of Inverness towards the Caley Thistle football ground and the Kessock Bridge. The early part of the tour was over the Black Isle on the A9 north past Kessock. On and over the Cromarty bridge, still on the A9 by passing Evanton, Alness and Tain. All the time, John and Karen were talking away. They were very close thought the Big Blue Bus and as though Cybil had read his thoughts, she whispered "Are they more than friends?" Ding, ding, ding. "Oh! I think so" said the Big Blue Bus "I really think so." With a quiet toot, toot, toot he whispered

"I hope so." There was a big smile on his radiator.
Just then, there was a loud 'wooowoah, wooowoah. The Big Blue Bus looked over and saw Travis the train roaring north, just as they were.

"Good Morning" said Travis "Good day. Are you two having fun, where are you going?" Wooowoah, wooowoah.

"No idea" said Cybil "we don't know. It's a mystery trip. Ding, ding, ding, so we can't tell you. Only John knows."

The Big Blue Bus went toot, toot, toot and added a long tooooot. "That's right, only John knows."

John and Karen laughed at the three of them and John put his foot on the accelerator and the Big Blue Bus picked up speed. Travis yelled across the fields "Beat you to Helmsdale, Big Blue Bus. Do you want to try and beat me?"

"Oh! A race" said Cybil "will we win Big Blue Bus?"

"I doubt it" said the Big Blue Bus "Travis has no traffic to worry about and we do and, to be honest, I think safety is a better option. Don't worry though, we can beat him to Thurso because he has to go to Kinbrace then Forsinard and across open country to Scotsdalder and then Georgemas Junction, so that adds a bit of time to his journey. The scenery is really pretty that way so his passengers will have a good time too."

Travis disappeared in the distance, he was sure to get to Helmsdale first now.

The passengers were busy taking photos of the views, click, click, click, clicking every few seconds. Video cameras whirled and sounded like flies buzzing in a bottle. 'Zzzzzzzz, zzzzzzzz'.

One man let out a loud laugh and then another said "The bends and hills of the Berriedale near Newport and Borgue, still on the A9, were like riding on the wild mouse roller coaster at Southsea in England." "I think they could be worse" said his wife Tracey "I would close my eyes if it wasn't for the wonderful views."

It took just about three hours to reach Thurso but before they went into the town John turned right onto the A 386 heading towards their first stop at Castle Town Slate and Stone Museum, right on the shore of Dunnet Bay. Visitors can wander all around the site and visit the museum where they learn that stone was dug from the hills and shipped to all corners of the world for buildings and field dividers. Many of which can be seen in the fields all around this area to this day. Life must have been very difficult then for everyone.

The Big Blue Bus sighed and said "Toot, toot, toot," before having a very welcome rest. "Me too" said Cybil and a soft ding, ding, ding, was heard by everyone as they got off the Big Blue Bus.

They spent two hours there and the passengers were full of stories of things they had seen and what they had learnt and spoke of very little else as John drove the Big Blue Bus back to Thurso where they would be staying the night in the Pentland Hotel. The passengers would enjoy an evening meal and maybe a wander around Thurso, then a good night's sleep before continuing their mystery tour in the morning.

As John parked the Big Blue Bus at the coach park not too far away, Karen took Cybil off and with John began to stroll back to the hotel. "Goodnight" said the Big Blue Bus. "Toot, toot, toot." "Goodnight" said Cybil. "Ding, ding, ding." The following day's weather was much like yesterday's and promised to be nicer in the afternoon.

The Big Blue Bus woke up to see a blurred image through sleepy headlights, just in front of him. "Is that who I think it is?" he said. Then using his head lamp wipers he cleared his eyes. "Oh, My!" he said "It's Morton." Toot, toot, toot. "Morton" he said loudly. "Morton the motorbike. Wake up. It's me, the Big Blue Bus."

Morton the motorbike shook as he started out of his sleep, revved up his engine which gave a solid motorbike sound that went bruuum, bruuum, bruuum. "Hi there, Big Blue Bus. How are you?"

"I'm fine" said the Big Blue Bus "I assume that you are Ok as you're all the way up here from Nairn. That's a long way for an old motorbike like you."

"I beg your pardon" said Morton "I'll have you know, that I might be a little beyond my best but I still have a lot of good miles left in me. Listen to this." With a loud bruuum, bruuum, bruuum he revved his 500cc engine up to its limit. He didn't keep it going long though and slowly but surely he slowed down and calmed down along with a bit of a cough and a splutter. "Well, not as sweet as I used to be eh! Still it's nice to be here."

"It is" said the Big Blue Bus.

"Where are you off to?" asked Morton.

"No idea" said the Big Blue Bus its John's secret. What about you?"

"Me? Oh! I'm off to John O'Groats for a picnic for the afternoon then I suppose the run back home down the A9, so when I see you next, you can let me know where you went."

"Toot, toot, toot" said the Big Blue Bus "no problem. I'll tell you everything."

Minutes later John came along and greeted the Big Blue Bus and proceeded to carry out his safety checks and afterwards he got into the cab and started the engine. Gently together they made their way back to the hotel to pick up the passengers. John still kept their destination secret, which annoyed the Big Blue Bus a little and he let out a slightly angry 'toooot!

The passengers were a talkative lot and the Big Blue Bus only just heard Cybil say "'ding, ding, ding and good morning," as Karen brought her on board.

"Morning" he said "this group are so loud I only just heard you. Toot, toot, toot."
John turned the steering wheel and headed out of Thurso, westward on the A 836.

I wonder, thought the Big Blue Bus, where will our next adventure take us?

MY EYES WEEP.

My eyes are weary

Tired of looking

Sometimes they cry with no sleep

My eyes are sleepy

But no sleep comes to me

That's what makes my eyes weep

My brain keeps ticking

I know no thinking

No plan comes together

For me to rest

Long time lying

Persistent trying

No rest for me in my bed

Snuggled up

quilt around my head

I turn over time after time

Trivial matters cloud my mind

I am not dead

My brain hurts

It goes round and round

No solace have I found

My eyes are weary

Of life's pain

Of times gone past

In which nothing can last

In my mind's eye sleep moved away

I grow old, alas, I know the end

We all do until the morning

Weary

Hole in the sky.

The problem was that there was no time. There never is. It just seems to fly by. Still I have no choice, just have to keep going I suppose. The weather was pretty bad. His twin-engined plane was weaving and dropping but it was fitted with the best of equipment and flying was his business, had been for years.

He sat back a little in his seat and recalled his past, how he saved his hard earned money in the army for nearly twenty years, then, afterwards as a mercenary in Africa, that paid a lot better but the danger was twice as bad.

He then let out a little laugh and recalled the time he tried his hand at bar keep, what a joke that was, different woman virtually every night, work until Two in the morning, then sleep for a few hours then up and back to clean up, open up again at ten in the morning and on until six o'clock. Then he got an hour's break, then back for the slog until the end of the day, day after day.What a laugh! For pennies too. Again he just laughed quietly to himself, inside.

However when he realised some of his staff had been, what he called adjusting the tills, he had made a decision to sell up and take up flying.

It didn't take him long to get his licence and very soon he was flying solo, so the next step was to own his own plane. That done, he went through the rigmaroles of being able to service it and fly it for, as yet unthought of, business reasons.. Then a place to keep it and some where to live, etc. etc.

The list went on but eventually he had got himself sorted all round. He had moved to the north of Scotland and had landed a contract job with a mail company delivering mail to the distant islands. Now and then he had a passenger or two, cash only though, he wasn't really supposed to carry them while he was carrying mail. Right now he was flying solo on a flight to one of the outer islands when he had flown into this dirty weather. A huge flash followed by a thunderous bang snapped him back to reality, the plane lurched sideways and dropped like a stone," Jesus", he screamed out loud,"what the hell?" All his body, limbs and brain were working furiously to regain control. Seconds past, which seemed like hours. However, slowly but surely, he regained control and steadied his flight. He quickly ran a check over his dials, fuel, height, position finder and as he went to move along the dials he was dragged back to the position finder. He was well off course. He made the necessary adjustments and slowly bought the plane back on course. The storm still raged and he had an image of himself hitting a mountain or crash landing onto a road in the wilds. He always imagined he would survive that one. Again he was snapped back to reality as the wind caught him sideways on and seemed it was doing its best to turn him off course, he turned more into the wind to get back on course and immediately lost some air speed. Oh boy this is not going to be fun he thought, he looked out of his starboard window, it was pitch black, only the sudden flashes of lighting bouncing off the edges of the clouds gave him some vision but that was for just seconds. Looking back to the front the rain still smashed against the screen virtually cutting off his vision ahead.

I'm flying virtually blind he whispered. Arms and legs were hurting badly, his head was pounding, every sinew straining to keep straight ahead, I should have turned back as I hit this damn storm. Me and my honesty and loyalty, yeah I will get the mail through boss, just like the pony express, nothing will stop the mail getting through, yeah right he whispered.

The lightning flashed right across his flight path and he let out another oath, one he wouldn't normally use but he felt the circumstances called for it. He flew on.

He lent forward to check his air speed and fuel gauge. Air speed and fuel versus the wind, rain and the distance. He thought well only time will tell with that one. Again he was drawn back into his past and recalled a field of battle in Africa. Now that was tough, he thought, pinned down for over an hour by rebels. He was supposed to stop them but when he and his pals tried, they realised these boys were skilled and well armed. He remembered the small child who run into the line of fire, both sides eased off the warfare for a few seconds for fear of killing the boy and he took a chance and ran off towards the wee man. Some rebels opened fire but he continued to the lad, He could hear the shouting for a cease fire from both sides but some die hard rebels would hear nothing of it and just wanted him dead. He grabbed the boy then weaving as he ran got back into his defence position diving for cover still holding the lad, a cheer went up from both sides but still the firing went on. He still don't know if that boy survived but he did and got out as soon as he could. He'd had enough..

A sudden lurch of the plane pulled him into concentration mode and he went back to the battle in hand against dear old mother nature. Well she is not so nice sometimes and this particular time seemed to have it in for him.

Again another check of fuel and speed and then a flash

of light but this time it was blue ,sky blue. "Jesus where was that? It was quickly gone but he knew that it came some way off , on his port side away from his destination but not so far off. It looked like a hole in the sky. Blue sky might mean the end of this bloody storm he thought, maybe I should just head that way. It might lead to safety but what about this bloody mail? He flew on.

Another sudden drop needed his top skill to correct and he had a gut wrenching feeling that he may just not come through this little battle.

His brain now was in frantic action with thoughts of his past and his war with the storm but somehow his past seemed to win and he recalled his first love. Susan, right from school she was to him the sweetest girl he knew and often found him in a fight with other boys for her attention but he won and eventually when they were in their late teens they got married. Oh how he loved her and the wee baby boy that followed shortly after the wedding. Memories flashed though his mind of holidays, trips away, billets in Germany and in many other countries and of chicken pox, yes chicken pox, he hadn't had them so when his boy caught them and passed them on to him, yeah that was a wee laugh he thought, weeks on leave and in quarantine with every one laughing at his demise. When Susan got pregnant again she returned to Britain to have the child, she also took Simon his boy, so for some weeks he was alone. One day his senior officer called for him and he was given the dreadful news that his wife and son were killed in a car accident, the baby could not be saved, he had a dreadful time mourning , bad dreams ugly scenes in bars when he was drunk falling out with friends and family but he got through it with

81

more than a little prayer now and then. He realised he was crying but he didn't care. From that day onward he had always done his best for anyone who he knew or met, either in peace time or combat. He often put his life on the line to prove his point that he would not be down hearted by such tragedy. Back to the fight in hand and again another scare as he looked at the fuel gauge and mentally tried to work out if he could make his destination, a quick shiver went through him as he realised that it was going to be very close , will he make it or not?, he could not be sure.

Again a flash of sky, light blue but this time it seemed a lot nearer and more to his nose than over to his port side. Just maybe I will beat this storm he said to himself but was shocked as another shudder and sudden drop of about three hundred feet meant he almost wet himself and again had to fight to keep his plane flying. He pulled back on the stick to gain height and pulled it over gently to realign his course, using his feet to move the rudder to keep him flying straight. He flew on.

That last little hole in the sky might just have been my last hope, maybe I should have flown for it he thought but I didn't so I will just have to get on with it.

Rain still pounded the windscreen and the wind howled the louder around him and his mind took him back to the short trip with the navy for an exercise. All went well for the first day but on the second a storm front hit and many a man was sea sick and conditions worsened quickly, he was ok and spent most of his time comforting his mates and generally helping out.

One soldier he knew well took a walk up the ladder to the deck and was promptly swept to the side railings and just managed to hang on, he had followed and bravely crawled out to the struggling soldier and pulled him to safety. His senior officer had seen what he had done and when they returned to the main land put his name forward for a bravery medal, he didn't want it really, just glad the soldier hadn't died.

He checked his instruments and stretched his arms and legs one at a time to relieve the aches.

Almost there according to my calculations, he thought I might just as well have a look downstairs to see if anything is visible. He pushed the stick forward and the plane responded and slowly lost height. Now the wind seemed to be pushing him from behind and his plane picked up speed, weaving and dropping even quicker. He fought like hell to keep control. Suddenly he had a view of the ground fast rushing up to meet him and with all his might he pulled back on the stick to try and regain height, powered up the engine more and pulled over to port to miss the up and coming hill ahead. It was almost as if he had touched the ground as trees and hills flew by the windows.

Just as he thought this is it, he caught a glimpse of the road leading to the airfield and turned towards it ,still fighting the raging storm. He tapped his instrument panel and wondered why the altimeter didn't give his correct height, must have been affected by the lightning he thought, no point looking at the fuel gauge that had long since been in the red zone. Now he had the road in sight and carried out his landing routine, his emergency landing routine that is. He thought, no ordinary landing this. Gently he eased the stick forward. "Wheels down he aimed for the road. A sudden upsurge of gale force wind got under him and was virtually trying to lift him back up but he fought on and pushed on down to his target, the road.

There was the airfield a few miles ahead," I might just make it" he said out loud, "Come on babe he yelled at his plane, come on!." Then the very worst noise any pilot can hear is the fuel empty warning, it was now ringing loud and clear in his cab, his starboard engine cut out and the plane headed down. Once again he got control and realised he was only a few hundred metres from touch down. Now he was cheering himself along but slammed back to reality once again when his port engine cut out. Now he was virtually helpless as the plane glided downwards at a pretty fast rate of knots. The ground came up very quickly to meet him as his wheels touched the road surface just short of the airfield's runway. It was all over so quickly and as he walked away from the plane said to himself out loud that the mail got though. "yeah just like the pony express!"

He stood on a wee bank at the side of the road and turned to watch the drama a hundred meters away. A fire engine and ambulance roared by him as he watched the burning wreckage by the airfield fence and the people running around. It was then he realised that a man stood beside him and he turned to see who it was. A second or so later he looked back to the crash site and said, I didn't make it did I?

" No" said the tall man in a white suit who then held out his hand, "Come on." he said, "Your wife and children are waiting. They turned together and walked to the brightly lit stairway that led up to the hole in the sky.

I am but a man

Shuffled my feet through dead leaves lying
Chin on my chest eyes closed fast
In my heart was the fear of the future I'm vying
As I walked through the trees autumn brown

I am but a man in the winter of life
But I carry a burden so vast
As spring reaches summer and flowers do bloom
It's on through that summer to last

Then on again through more golden days
To ones that are crystallised white
Right through that summer and on to the next
Walking on through my new gateway of life

As you walk beside me my burden is lighter
We hold hands as we stroll on our way
It's you that carries me and makes me stand tall
Of my burden I am frightened no more

A problem once shared is halved so they say
Many a friend of ours heard the news
Each one I love and all held dear in my mind
Between them all, they lifted my heart

I face the sun of tomorrow and on
Alone I'm no longer standing
With you I have seen a bright new beginning
The battle I am in, I am winning

I shuffled my feet through dead leaves lying
My head held high, my eyes wide open
The fear in my heart it was waning
As I walked through the trees autumn brown.

Tis but a curse.

Tears of blood weep from the pores of man
As he thrashes and frails through the heavy waters of life
He cares not for the space he has
But longs for the space of others
Only, why he wants that space,
he does not know
He marches on through
with a murky view of life
Then creates a floor of blood
On his life's carpet which he weaves
if it flows
He does not see his own blood in the pattern he makes
It is the curse of man that he is blind
Blind to the needs of others
His ears closed to the screams
He is cursed with religion or beliefs
This feeds his passion for a glorious death
Death of another or himself
It is hoped he will find peace
or glory thereafter
All men fail to see that while one man thinks this
Another is thinking the same
It is a curse that neither can see nor abide each other's wish
So both will die and their dreams die with them
It's a curse for a man to bear.
He will carry it to his grave.
For that is where we all go
Tis. But a curse..